Massachusetts Sabbath-School Society

Charley and the blind man, and other stories

Massachusetts Sabbath-School Society

Charley and the blind man, and other stories

ISBN/EAN: 9783743309401

Manufactured in Europe, USA, Canada, Australia, Japa

Cover: Foto ©Andreas Hilbeck / pixelio.de

Manufactured and distributed by brebook publishing software
(www.brebook.com)

Massachusetts Sabbath-School Society

Charley and the blind man, and other stories

Charley and Carlo.

CHARLEY

AND

THE BLIND MAN,

AND OTHER STORIES.

WRITTEN FOR THE MASSACHUSETTS SABBATH-SCHOOL SOCIETY,
AND APPROVED BY THE COMMITTEE OF PUBLICATION.

BOSTON:
MASSACHUSETTS SABBATH-SCHOOL SOCIETY.
DEPOSITORY, NO. 13 CORNHILL.

CONTENTS.

————◆————

CHARLEY AND THE BLIND MAN.

ONE bright morning in early summer Charley whistled for his dog Carlo, who obeyed the summons by running up to his little master and jumping and frisking about, stopping now and then to give a short, sharp bark, and then jumping up on Charley and nearly throwing him down.

"O Carlo! be quiet, and behave like a sensible dog," said Charley. "I want to tell you that we are going to take a long walk this morning; we are going to my grandmother's, and I want you to be a very good Carlo, and not run after the chickens, nor worry the cows, nor frighten the birds, but come along by me and behave like a

well-bred dog;" and Charley stooped down
and patted and caressed his little favorite,
who by this time seemed nearly frantic with
delight.

Famous friends were these two, the boy
and his dog. Many were the rambles they
had together through the woods and over
the meadows, and by the little river and
away down to the village.

Charley's brother and sister were much
older than himself, and thus it happened
that Carlo became his almost constant com-
panion; and he had formed a habit of talking to him, as if he understood much more
of the English language than dogs are
generally supposed to be able to do. Carlo
could not answer Charley in so many words,
but he looked up very knowingly into his
face, as much as to say, "Ay, ay! I am glad
to hear you say so. We will go indeed, and
a capital time we will have, too;" and then
he barked and jumped more extravagantly,

if possible, than before. Just then Charley's mother called to him that the basket was ready that he was to take to his grandmother ; and he went into the house to get it, and to give his mother one more kiss before he started, for Charley was a great pet in his own home. His mother doted on her gentle boy ; and this morning, as she smoothed his curling hair, long and lovingly did she gaze on that young face that so vividly recalled the features of her own brother, who years ago bade her goodby and sailed away on the wide ocean, but who would never, nevermore return to her sisterly love. She at length placed the basket on his arm, and Charley and Carlo were fairly started on their important excursion — important to Charley, because the little fellow had never been so far from home before, unattended by any of the family.

No wonder Carlo was in high spirits that

bright June morning. Roses and honey-
suckles, and all sweet and beautiful flowers
were in bloom. Orioles and robins, red
birds and yellow birds, were taking part in
one grand chorus; and the bees, as they
helped themselves to the honey from all the
flowers, seemed to think they were all made
for *them*, and by their continual hum, hum,
announced that their mission on the earth
was a very important one indeed. And
then there were so many squirrels that
were running along on the fences and up
the trees — oh, it was very hard for Carlo
not to follow and catch them; but Charley
was continually reminding him that he was
not on a hunting expedition, and so, by
scolding and coaxing, he managed to keep
him pretty quiet by his side.

At length, on entering another road that
led directly to the village, Carlo suddenly
stopped, pricked up his ears and began to
growl, as if he saw something that displeased

him very much ; and Charley, looking round
for the cause of these hostile signals, saw
an old man with a cane, and he, too, had a
dog, — a little black dog (Carlo was brown
and white), — and the old man had one end
of a string in his hand, while the other end
was tied around the dog's neck. Charley
wondered what it all meant, and Carlo —
Charley's commands to the contrary — kept
up a low, muttering growl; but as the old
man came up to them with slow and feeble
step, Charley saw that he was blind, and at
first he felt, not exactly frightened, but a
little strange, as if he would like to hurry
on and get out of the way. But the poor
old man spoke to him in such a low voice,
and seemed altogether so harmless, that
Charley began to pity him very much, and
so he stopped and talked to him a little
while, — though Carlo said very plainly by
his manner, " If I were you I would keep
good company, or none at all." Dogs are

so proud, they think so much of dress and appearance, and are always ready to bark at shabby-looking people. The old man told Charley that he was very poor, and that he lived in the almshouse, — the large red house on the other side of the village, — that he was sick, too ; and that on warm days it was a great pleasure to go out with his faithful dog and breathe the sweet, fresh air, and enjoy the warm sunshine, and listen to all the music of birds and brooks and bees. He spoke cheerfully, but Charley thought his life must seem like one long night, and he remembered the ten cents he had in his little purse, which he took out and begged the old man to accept. He then bade him good-morning, and walked on ; but he could think of little else than the blind old man, whose best earthly friend was his dog, and somehow everything seemed changed. A little while ago and the world seemed full of joy and song, but now he thought there must be a great deal of sorrow and darkness mingled with the brightness and happiness of life. He shut his eyes and tried to walk a little way, that he might have a small experience in blindness; but he was glad enough to open them again; and then he thought that for more than sixty years the old man had groped his way in darkness. He soon reached his grandmother's. She lived in a small, low, brown house, and on one side of the door was a rose-bush that had climbed and climbed till it had reached the very top of the house, and this morning it was covered with hundreds of beautiful white roses that filled the air with delicious fragrance. Everything inside the house was so clean and old-fashioned and queer, that it had a great charm for Charley. He thought the little odd-shaped closets, and the great old kitchen, and the white, uncarpeted floors were all in much better taste than the mod-

ern improvements of his father's house.
And then, to trot round after his grandmother, and watch her when she turned the
cheeses and stamped the butter, and, best
of all, when she made doughnuts, — not the
genteel, light-colored, hard little rings that
go by that name in these modern days, but
the real genuine article that grandmothers
used to regale us with — brown, round, and
pulpy. Charley's grandmother, you must
know, attended to all these things herself,
although she had more than numbered her
threescore years and ten. Still, Charley
did not like to hear her talk about dying,
which she was rather apt to do, particularly
when he admired her long white hair, which
Charley thought was as handsome as molten
silver. Then she would shake her head
and say, " Yes, yes ; I have seen many long
years, and I must die very soon." Charley
comforted himself by thinking she had told
him the same thing ever since he could

remember, and as she never had died, perhaps she wouldn't till he grew up to be a man.

When Charley and Carlo were walking home that afternoon, as they came near the baker's shop in the village, whom do you think they saw sitting on a bench by the wayside? The old blind man. He had bought some gingerbread with the money Charley gave him, which he was sharing with his dog. As soon as the old man heard his step, he recognized his little friend of the morning, and Charley stopped to have a chat with him; but I am sorry to say Carlo kept growling all the time, though in a low tone, as if he were half-ashamed of himself.

When Charley reached home that night, the very first thing he told his mother was about the old man who could not see, never had looked on faces that he loved, never had seen how beautiful and glorious God

had made the earth and sky. After the
little boy was in bed that night, his mother
came and sat by the bedside, and told him
a story from the Bible. She said that one
Sabbath evening, as Jesus was coming out
of the temple, where he had very much
offended the Jews, — indeed, they were so
angry they tried to stone him, — he saw a
man that had been blind from his birth.
And the compassionate Saviour pitied him
so much that he determined to cure him ;
and he spit on the ground, and made clay,
and rubbed it on the eyes of the blind man,
and then commanded him to go and wash
in a certain pool. As soon as he obeyed
Jesus, his eyes were opened and he saw.
Charley wondered how the world and the
people looked to the man who was thus
so suddenly and wonderfully cured. His
mother told him the Bible did not say ; and
then he asked her if it said nothing of the
love and gratitude the man must ever after

have cherished towards the Almighty friend who had done for him more than all the wisdom and riches of the world could possibly do. His mother advised him to read the story for himself. He could certainly find if the man became the friend and disciple of Jesus, and he would also find other interesting stories of blind people to whom Jesus, when on earth, gave sight.[1] She told him, besides, that she thought the little boys and girls and men and women who had never been blind had vastly more reason to love and obey the Saviour than those who had been blind part of their lives, and then had sight given them. Charley thought his mother was right, but he appeared to be very much interested in blind people. There was something about the old man that had left a strong and pleasant impression on Charley. He could not tell what it

[1] Compare John ix., Mark viii. 22–26, x. 46–52; Luke xviii. 85–43; Matt. xx. 30–34, xii. 22, xxi. 14.

was; but in his loneliness and sightlessness the old man had thought so much of the bright world where he knew he had an abiding home, and had prayed with such a submissive and believing heart, that God had given him so much of his Spirit that even a child, though he talked with him but a very little while, discerned and was blessed by the heavenly influence.

The next day was the Sabbath, and Charley took his little Testament and looked over it very carefully, and when he found a place where it said anything about the miracles that Christ wrought on the blind, he put in a mark; and his sister, seeing what he was about, joined him in his study, and by patiently comparing the story of one Evangelist with another, they could tell their mother at night all that has been recorded of those wonderful miracles. Little friend, can you tell?

A week or two after his visit to his grand-

mother's the hay-makers came, and Charley
and Carlo were as busy and happy as the
live-long day.   Very early in the morning
they were in the hay-field, watching the
men as they sharpened their scythes and
cut down the tall grass, running and frol-
icking about in the new-mown hay, until
sometimes the men would get cross, and
call out that they were in the way and doing
mischief.   Charley knew very well how to
bring back their good-nature.   He would
go into the house and return with a bounti-
ful luncheon of cakes and milk, and after
the tired mowers had partaken of this refreshment, it was surprising to see how suddenly amiable and indulgent they became.
When the hay was "spread" and "turned"
and "raked," Charley felt he was quite an
important character ; for he had a pitchfork
and rake suited to his size and strength, and
he worked away with a hearty good-will, and
felt that his help was of great importance.

2

Whether it was so or not, I am not at lib
erty to say.

But a sad accident befell Charley one
afternoon in the hay-field. In trying to get
into the cart that had come to take the hay
to the barn, he stepped on the wheel while
the cart was in motion; his foot slipped
through the spokes, and the wheel in turning gave his leg a terrible wrench. The
little boy uttered one sharp cry of pain, and
fell. His father and the workmen were
quickly at his side, anxious to know how
badly he was hurt; but all he could say
was to moan out, in piteous tones, " My leg!
my leg! " They carried him to the house,
and when the doctor came he said the leg
was broken. Poor Charley! he received a
great deal of pity and tenderness; — he was
such a little fellow, so much younger and
smaller than any one else in the family.
Well, the doctor " set " the broken leg, and
it was a very painful operation, it was so

badly wrenched and bruised; and when it was done, and they laid him on his little cot, you would almost have thought he was dead, he looked so pale, and was obliged to lie so perfectly still. All night long his mother sat by his side, reading and telling him stories, trying to amuse him, so he might not think so much of his aching leg; or, as grown people say, "getting him out of himself." But when the morning came he fell asleep, and after that first night of suffering he had little pain in his leg; but he was obliged to lie very still for a long time. And in all these weary days a very afflicted dog was Carlo, seldom leaving the bedside of his little master, but lying on a mat at the foot of the bed, looking up into Charley's face with such a meek, pitying expression that people could hardly help laughing, and Charley thought they were less human than the dog. Charley's little friends were also very kind, coming to see him, and bringing their new books and toys, trying to make the days pass pleasantly, — those beautiful summer days, when little boys and girls so seriously object to being housed; when it seems so important that they should be out of doors watching how the currants and gooseberries are ripening in the garden, looking after the calves and chickens, picking the berries that are waiting for them in such abundance in the woods and by the waysides, — the beautiful summer, when hundreds of happy children are laying up " sunny memories " for coming years. We pity Charley, shut up in his little room in this happy time, and breathe a wish that he will soon be out in the pleasant sunshine.

Charley was very much surprised one morning when his mother told him that the blind man was at the door — came to inquire how the little boy was getting along who had hurt himself so badly, and who

had been so kind to him. Charley begged
that he might come in at once. He was
pleased that the old man remembered him,
and had walked so far to learn how he was;
so he welcomed him very politely, and
Carlo had the good manners not to growl
this time; but if the *whole* truth must be
told, he was far from giving him a cordial
greeting, — very different from the fawning
way with which he was wont to meet the
rich and well-dressed people who came to
see his little master. O Carlo! who would
have thought there was so much pride in
your composition? Learn a lesson from
your mistress, Charley's mother. See how
kindly she treats the old man, how respect-
fully she listens as he tries to entertain her
sick boy, and is telling the story of his own
life — a story that is often told. When young
he lived in prosperity and happiness; father,
mother, brothers and sisters all pitying him
for the great calamity that had deprived him

of the many, many pleasures which sight affords. It was not till he had passed early manhood that death came to his home, and came so often that one by one was borne away, till all were sleeping in the grave, and he alone was left. And then, one cold windy night, a fire broke out in the village, and his own house, with many of his neighbors', was burnt; and with the house all the rest of his property was swept away, and he was obliged to find a home in the almshouse in the town where his father had once held a position of influence.

All who heard the old man talk always noticed one thing, — there was no bitterness nor murmuring in his words. "It was all right," he said. God had taken away those blessings, and now the time was short that he would have to stay on the earth; his strength was failing day by day, and soon he should go *home* to his eternal home in the skies.

The old man was persuaded to stay till he was thoroughly rested and had partaken of some refreshment; and then, as the day was very warm, Charley's father said one of the men would take him back to the almshouse in the wagon. The two friends parted very kindly, for they had taken a great fancy to each other — the old man and the little boy, with such a long distance of years between them. You must not imagine because Charley talked to his dog in such a wise way, and was so fond of the company of an old blind pauper, that he was a little old man himself. No; he was full of play and fun. He had as brave a heart, and as merry a laugh as any boy. Nothing delighted him more than stories of courage and daring, stories of the heroism and brave endurance of soldiers, and of the perils of the sea, and the narrow escapes and wonderful adventures of travellers in distant and uncivilized countries, where wild animals still roamed in the woods, giving an opportunity to huntsmen to try their skill at larger game than rabbits and partridges. Oh to kill a bear! Charley thought that achievement would make any boy immortal; and the picture in his brother's history of Putnam's going down into the den after the wolf — Charley had looked at it and heard the story hundreds of times.

The old man repeated his visit to Charley. The little black dog running on before, and the bowed figure of the old man following after, were often seen turning their steps towards the handsome house where Charley had his happy home, and where a warm welcome was always waiting for his friend. Sometimes he brought early sweet apples from the farm at the almshouse, sometimes luscious berries that little children had gathered in the woods and given to the gentle old man who could not see, and had nothing to give in return but grateful words and his earnest prayers that God would bless them with happy and prosperous lives.

At length Charley was able to be out again. At first he walked with a crutch, but in a few days *that* was laid aside, and he used a cane instead, and then he dispensed with *all* such helps, and his step was as strong and free as on that pleasant morning when he and Carlo took that ever-to-be-remembered walk to his grandmother's.

One morning, when his father had taken Charley out for a drive, he proposed that they should go to the almshouse and see why the blind man had stayed away so long; for it had been many days since they had seen him, and they feared he was ill, or some accident had happened to him. They were correct in their surmises, for when they reached the almshouse they found the old man was too ill to go out for his accustomed walks. He was lying on his bed,

where he had been for more than a week.
But his pale, sick face lighted up with a
very bright smile as he welcomed his visitors. He thanked them again and again for
their kindness in coming to see him, and
parted with them with repeated and fervent God bless you's.

The woman who took care of him told
Charley that everybody was kind to the
poor man, his life was so gentle and holy;
and he tried so constantly to know and do
the will of God, that all who knew him felt
the influence of his godly life. He had
great power to attract little children. She
thought it strange that a sightless old man,
so bowed with years and sorrows, should
have such a charm for bright young children, it mattered not whether they were
rich or poor.

On one of those beautiful October days,
when the white clouds are sailing about so
slowly up in the sky, and the winds are so

very still that it is almost impossible to believe there ever will be another storm or tempest, Charley and his brother were out in the orchard picking up the red and yellow apples that lay scattered so thickly under the big old trees. Suddenly the bell of the village church began to toll, and Charley knew that a funeral was passing through the streets. Just then a neighbor came along, and said the blind man that lived in the almshouse was dead, and they were carrying him to the burying-ground to lay him beside the friends who had slumbered there so many years. And so the long night of his life was over, and he had gone to eternal day. That poor old man, with no money, no kindred, no home but the almshouse, had passed away; but he had left behind him the power of a holy life. Many had been won by his example to a life of submission and trust in the Divine will.

As for Charley, he grew up with more faith and love in his heart towards God and man from the influence of that good old man whom he had known when only a small boy; and years after, when he was no longer a little boy, but a tall, broad-shouldered man, he had a headstone put up at the blind pauper's grave, with this inscription: "The Lord shall be unto thee an everlasting light, and thy God thy glory."

HISTORY

OF

FIDELITY AND PROFESSION.

AN ALLEGORY.

FIDELITY AND PROFESSION.

---◆---

ONCE upon a time there lived a certain king, who had very large possessions in a distant part of the world; but for a time he sent his son to dwell in a small island, which that Prince had, in a measure, subdued to himself from the hands of a wicked and cruel tyrant. The inhabitants of this island were exceedingly numerous and very active, and of a smaller size than the race of men.

After remaining some time in this island, the king's son was called away to his distant possessions. But before he went, he gave many orders to his servants. Among these were two boys, to whom he had shown extraordinary kindness, and who had al-

ways professed great attachment to him.
The names of these two boys were Fidelity and Profession.　The Prince called
them to him as he sat in the hall of his
palace, which opened into a garden, or
rather, I should say, into two gardens,— for
a winding brook ran through the centre of
the garden, in front of the palace, and separated it into two equal parts ; and as each
part was laid out exactly in the manner of
the other, I shall content myself with de-
scribing the one, as the Prince led the two
children through it.

He first took them to a dark recess in the
garden, where, from a rock overgrown with
moss, dropped a small spring of very cold
water.　Dark trees and shrubs overhung the
rock, and shut out every ray of sunshine; a
few pale flowers hung their pensive heads
over the water.　A cold and damp feeling
chilled the boys as they entered the place,
and they seemed glad to get out of it, par-

ticularly Profession; but Fidelity noticed that the grass near the water was particularly green, and many lilies of the valley scented the air with their perfume, at a very small distance from the spring. And when he had moved a few yards from the spot, he saw a very bright light playing upon the water, as it ran from the rock into the brook which bounded either garden. "That light does not come from the sun," said Fidelity, "for it is hid behind a cloud."

Then the Prince bade him look up; and he saw, opposite the rock, a grassy mount, upon which stood a cross. Round the top of this cross there rested a light brighter than the sun at noon-day. At the foot of the mount several lambs were lying asleep. Every kind of sweet and refreshing flowers grew on the sloping side of the mount. At its foot opened a well-cultivated wilderness, where shrubs from every climate of the world were planted, and grew in luxu-

riance.   Vines and fruit trees were here
loaded with fruit; flowers of spring and
summer and autumn were scattered irregu-
larly on the soft velvet turf, and paths in-
numerable wound among the trees.   These
paths again met in a delicate little lawn,
which, by the easiest and most agreeable
ascent, led to an eminence where was
planted a delightful arbor.

Fidelity and Profession were charmed
with the appearance of this garden. " Surely, sir," said Profession, " you are not going
to give us these gardens ? "

" We are not worthy of them," answered
Fidelity.

" I am willing to hope," replied the
Prince, " that you are so sensible of your
obligations to me, that you will prove your
love by taking care of these gardens, if I
intrust them to you."

" The task is too easy," said Profession.

" We ought," replied Fidelity, " if they

are intrusted to us, to keep them in the most beautiful order."

"The employment," answered the Prince, "which I give to you during my absence, and in doing which you will show your love to me, would be in itself exceedingly easy and pleasant, were it not that the persons who are to labor in it, the inhabitants of this island, are of so perverse and disorderly a character, that you will find the utmost difficulty in making them obey you. Yet I will not leave you comfortless; I will send a friend and adviser and helper to you, who will be your director in all your difficulties. But come now with me, and I will show you what you have to do; and I will tell you the names of the different parts of your garden."

First he led them to the dark rock where the spring was dropping, and the trees were planted in gloomy shade. "This," said he, "is the Grotto of Repentance. This spot

your servants will not love; but you must
be exceedingly strict with them, and insist
upon their laboring here."

He then led them to the mount where
the cross stood: and he told them that it
was called the Mount of Faith or Salvation,
and that a certain number of their servants
must always wait there, and that if they
did so, the friend he promised them would
be at hand to assist them.

From thence he conducted them into the
wilderness, or vineyard, as it was sometimes
called, of Charity, whose paths, though so
numerous, all lead from the same mount,
and again meet in one spot, the pleasant
plain, which took them to the little hill and
bower. Here the Prince sat down, and bid
the boys sit at his feet.

"From no part of the island," said he,
" is there a finer prospect to be seen than
from this bower. Look beyond the sea roll-
ing at our feet, and you will behold a part

of my dominions with which you are not yet acquainted, — a land that is very far off, a goodly land, where there are many mansions, where the tree of life flourishes, and the river of the water of life flows; where flowers bloom and never fade; where sin troubles not joy, and death contends not with life. Love me, my children, and keep my commandments," continued the Prince, "while I am away, and when I return I will take you to this land."

Profession answered, that he could not bear to hear of the Prince leaving him.

Fidelity kissed the hand of his Prince, upon which he dropped a silent tear.

"The name of this arbor is Hope," said the Prince, "and your servants will be willing enough to work here : but you must never permit any to be employed in this arbor who have not labored in the Grotto of Repentance, the Hill of Faith, and the Vineyard of Charity."

" I understand," said Fidelity, " that our
servants in this work are to be the people
of this island, a pigmy race in size, but very
difficult to govern ; active indeed, in some
respects, but in other respects very indolent;
they will be continually begging to be re-
leased from their work and allowed some
rest."

" As to that," replied the Prince, " I know
the infirmity of their nature, and have provided for it. In every part of this garden
I have scattered here and there resting-
places, where they may sit down and gather
the flowers of domestic love and innocent
pleasure, and where they may enjoy refreshing sleep when fatigued, and the highest of
all pleasures the friend I have provided for
you will afford them when it is good for
them. He will bring with him one of the
harps of paradise, and they will sit at his
feet charmed into calm and silent attention when he touches the strings of it, and

sing them the songs of Zion, whispering to them, in words unutterable by mortals, the language of celestial Peace, the language of the COMFORTER."

The Prince paused, and Fidelity hung on his words. At last he said to him, "I have only to ask you one question : will this friend you promise us never leave us ?"

"No," replied the Prince, "if you are mindful of my words, and if you seek his presence, and never grieve him. But," proceeded the Prince, "I have a caution to give you. Beyond these gardens there is a desert land. It is called the Land of Carnal Desire. It is bounded on one side by the uplands of Natural Pride, and on the other by the mountains of Despair. It is an evil land, and reserved for burning ; but your servants are so fond of this land, where they were born, that you will find the utmost difficulty to keep them out of it. Indeed, they will make such excuses, and will bring you such reasons, seemingly so wise and prudent, for going there, as will deceive yourselves, if you are not always on the watch. But remember, that on no account whatever are they to visit that country : they are never to leave this garden ; here is their place of labor. When I come back, my children, let me find you in these gardens, with your servants around you, at work, and in good order. The task may be hard ; but as your day is, so will be your strength ; and by keeping these my commandments, you will show your love to me, and you will become yourselves unspeakably happy."

In reply to this speech of the Prince, Profession assured him, in the strongest manner, of his attachment to him ; and declared that it should be the only business of his life to do his will during his absence.

Fidelity looked earnestly at his Prince, and answered, " Thou knowest, Lord, that

I love thee, but thou knowest also my infirmity."

The Prince having finished his directions, conducted each to a little mossy hut, placed at the upper end of each garden, called Watchfulness, from whence might be seen everything that passed in every part of the garden. Here he took his leave of them in a tender and affectionate manner; first, however, giving into their charge the servants who were to be their laborers.

These servants were very numerous — so numerous that I could hardly count them; very small in size, and so active, that their motions resembled those of the swiftest birds. While the Prince was in the garden, they hung round him, and they stood perfectly still for some minutes after he was gone; but in a very short time they were all in motion, and before Fidelity and Profession were aware of it, a great many of the laborers had left the garden, and had

settled themselves in a little town called
Earthly Melancholy; others were saunter-
ing along the Vineyard of Charity: and the
rest were fast asleep.

I shall for the present dwell chiefly upon
the history of Fidelity; and I shall, there-
fore, relate how, when things were in this
state, and, indeed, getting worse, the kind
friend whom the Prince had promised to
send to assist the boys came, in his extraordinary love to Fidelity, and gently touch-
ing him, brought to his remembrance those
things which the Prince had said to him.

Fidelity started up from his seat, and to
his great surprise perceived that most of
his servants had left the garden. With
tears in his eyes, he begged his kind friend
to show him where they were gone; and he
pointed out to him the larger part of them
amusing themselves in a spacious garden
belonging to the palace of Vain Hope,
which joined on one side to the town of
Earthly Melancholy.

"Oh! help me," cried Fidelity, "to re-call these wanderers. Oh, my Prince, my Prince! what an ungrateful child I have been!"

The inmost sigh of Fidelity was not ut-tered before, at the command of his friend, all his servants, with rapid obedience, ap-peared again in the garden; and, by the direction of his friend, Fidelity took up a little wand called Diligence, which he found in his hut, and drove all his servants to their proper places. They were none of them permitted for the present, on account of their late offence, to work in the Arbor of Hope; but were divided among the Grotto of Repentance, the Hill of Faith, and the Vineyard of Charity. Fidelity humbly and patiently, yet somewhat sadly, followed them with his wand all day, from time to time casting his eyes upon his friend, who stood by strengthening him.

Towards evening, when the sun was set-

ting amidst gold and purple clouds, this
friend, who delights in being the Comforter
of his people, and who would always be
their Comforter if they would entertain
him, led Fidelity and his servants to the
Hill of Hope ; and while Fidelity sat in the
arbor with his servants at his feet, he took
his harp of gold — celestial gold — and
played to them one of those melodies
which the ears of the worldly minded cannot hear, — one of those melodies which
tune to peace the soul of the patient suf-
ferer, which call to laborious action the
pastor laboring in foreign climes, — one of
those melodies which turn pain into ease,
death into life.

After this sweet evening, many days and
weeks passed away most delightfully ; for
while Fidelity kept his servants at the Hill
of Faith his friend never left him ; and
while *he* was with him all went well. By
his direction he constantly used the wand

of Diligence, and kept his servants working in their proper places. And their friend and Comforter not seldom ravished them to joy with his heavenly melodies; and at all times he whispered to them peace, — peace like that pleasant feeling which we taste when in spring we feel the beams of the warm sun, and hear the buzz of the early bee as he visits the fresh primrose and violet.

One evening, as Fidelity was sitting in his hut at his evening meal, Profession, whom he did not very frequently see, called upon him, and brought with him a basket of apples. They were exceedingly fair to look at, and Profession immediately offered one to Fidelity.

Fidelity ate it, and commended its flavor very highly, and being hungry, he helped himself to another. "You have excellent fruit in your garden," said Fidelity.

"These apples do not grow in my gar

den," answered Profession. " My servants
bring them for me out of an orchard called
Sensual Pleasure."

" That orchard," answered Fidelity, " is
in the land of Carnal Desire. Surely you
do not suffer your servants to go there. I
begin to repent of eating those apples. I
thought they came out of your garden."

" As to that," replied Profession, smiling,
" you need not disturb yourself, for I eat
of them daily ; and provided they are eaten
in moderation, they will do you no harm,
and your credit will not suffer by it."

" Ah ! " said Fidelity, " but I shall grieve
my Prince, for he has forbidden our having
anything to do with that country, or ever
permitting our servants to go there. Our
work lies in our garden."

" It is very true," replied Profession,
" that we must have our gardens in good
order when our Prince returns ; but it will
probably be some time before he comes ;

and, so that our work is done, we may surely have a little enjoyment in the meantime. Besides, I always make my servants do something in the garden every day; at least, I show them every part of the garden, and give them directions about what is to be done, and talk to them about the excellency and beauty of a well-ordered garden, so that when we begin to work in good earnest, they will know what to set about. And in general, they are pretty willing to listen, provided I let them have their liberty afterwards."

"Indeed," said Fidelity, alarmed, "I think you are in a very dangerous state. If you let these servants of yours have so much liberty, you will never get them in order, and it is quite uncertain when our Prince may come back. Besides, you cannot govern your servants yourself, and perhaps if you never ask the kind Friend that was promised us to come to your help now, he will not assist you at last."

" As to that," answered Profession, " I
am not afraid ; for I do not think so ill of
my servants as many people do. They
have, certainly, their faults ; but I think
there is a great deal of honesty and good-
nature among them, and I do not doubt
that, even without the help you speak of,
I shall be able to bring my garden into good
order when I set about it. And in the
meantime, I am far happier without the
constant presence of that person ; for, between friends, though I think it right, in
order to keep well among the King's servants, to say a good deal in praise of the
King, and his Son, and this Friend who is
as himself, yet I think their laws and commandments rather grievous, and their company has always been a burden to me."

" Indeed," replied Fidelity, " I am quite
of a different opinion. Ever since the
King's Son showed his love to us, in so wonderful a manner, while we were rebels, I

have loved him with the tenderest love, and found his company sweeter to me than honey and the honey-comb; and for his Friend I can truly say, that he is rightly named the Comforter, and when he is away from me my soul refuseth rest."

"And yet," answered Profession, "he requires you to give up a thousand pleasures: these blooming apples, which are my daily food, you do not dare to taste." Then he archly raised up his basket towards the face of Fidelity, and he, having allowed himself to taste them, felt such a desire for them that he could not help sighing.

Profession now laughed aloud, and wickedly mocking him, he said, "Since you dare not send for more, I will at least leave you these, and so farewell." With that he left him in haste.

Fidelity, though he had talked well to Profession, yet, as is sometimes the case on these occasions, had received more harm

4

than he had done good.   When Profession
was gone, he sat silently musing on what he
had heard, and the poison entered into his
soul.   He felt exceedingly unwilling to look
for his Friend, and tell him what had
passed; and though every night he spent
sometime with his servants at the Grotto
of Repentance and the Hill of Faith, he
now persuaded himself that the hour was
passed, and that his servants were too
weary for the purpose, and he laid himself
down on his bed to sleep.   And here, what
with the effect of the fruit he had eaten,
and what with musing on the words of
Profession, he tossed about sleepless and
uneasy.   He was hot and feverish, and in-
tolerably thirsty.   He got up to drink some
water.   It would have been well if he had
gone to the water in the Grotto of Repentance to assuage his thirst; but, alas! he
smelt the fruit in the basket which Profession had left, and persuading himself that

it was too late and too dark now to seek for anything cooling in his garden, he greedily devoured the apples, and reeled back to his bed, for they intoxicated like wine, and here he fell into a feverish and disturbed sleep.

A little after his usual time of rising, he awoke, though not refreshed, and he got up to see if his servants were at work; but he found only a few in the garden, fast asleep at the foot of the Mount of Faith. And looking further, he perceived that all the rest had escaped into the land of Carnal Desire, and were all feasting upon grapes which one named Self-Indulgence was giving them out of a hot-house.

Fidelity knew well that his servants loved to be in this place, and that he could not, without the utmost effort and difficulty, drive them from it; and as he felt exceedingly drowsy, he allowed himself to think that it would be better to finish his sleep before he set about a business so difficult.

So he lay down to sleep once more. He
awoke again about noon; but he thought
it was too hot to do anything with his servants: so again he lay down, and dozed
away a few more hours.

Evening at last came on. " Before the
sun sets," said Fidelity, " I will take a
view of my servants, and see where they
are ; and in the morning I will collect
them together. We shall not be the worse,
I hope, for one lost day."

So saying, he walked along every part
of his garden. It was desolate — without
one inhabitant, except the few who still lay
sleeping at the foot of the mount. A thousand little employments had been neglected:
the flowers had not been watered, the with-
ered blossoms had not been cleared away,
the ripe fruit had fallen unplucked. Fidelity thought of his Prince, and sighed.

" Well," said he, " I shall soon see my
servants : they are, no doubt, still eating

the grapes of Self-Indulgence." Fidelity
looked for them, but they were gone from
thence.

At last he saw a few of them straggling
about at a little distance from the hot-house,
handcuffed, however, and driven along by
a cross-looking fellow, called Sullenness.

" You may look after those servants of
yours," cried the man, seeing Fidelity, "but
you will never have them to work for you
in your garden : for I took them prisoners
while they were eating grapes in yonder
garden, and I have delivered most of them
up to my king, and these I am taking up to
him."

" And where are they ? " asked Fidelity.

" Look," said the man, " to that com-
mon, beyond which lie those dark hills.
Do you see yonder towers ? "

Fidelity looked, and saw many high and
narrow black towers.

" Those are prisons," said Sullenness;

" and the keepers of them are the children of the king of our land himself: they are named Unbelief, Enmity, Mistrust, Despair, Pride, Malice, Hatred; sturdy young men as you would wish to see. And I will venture to say, that you, with all your strength, will never get one of your servants out of their hands; so you may as well sit down contented without them."

Fidelity was like one in a palsy when he heard these words. He sat himself down on the ground, saying to himself, " What good will my life do me? Oh that I had never been born!"

Now Fidelity did not sit down near the Grotto of Repentance, nor the Hill of Faith, but as near as could be to the boundary of his garden; and his eyes raised on the mountains of Despair, at the foot of which his servants were imprisoned.

How long he would have sat here is uncertain, had he been left to himself; but his kind Friend, his Comforter, his Helper, of whom, indeed he had not bethought himself since he had tasted the fruit, mourned over him, and tenderly pitied him. He had, it is true, withdrawn himself from Fidelity, for he had grieved him, and he is not wont to stay with those who do not love his presence. He had retired to the thickest part of the garden, where Fidelity could not see him ; and now he was preparing to leave the garden altogether ; yet, before he went, he determined to make one attempt to recall Fidelity to the remembrance of the things that make for his peace. He had, over and over again, acted this kind part by Profession in vain, yet his long-suffering was not worn out. Unseen by Fidelity (although the moon had risen), he drew near to him, and while his fixed eyes rested on the mountains of Despair, he whispered in his ear, " Awake your servants who are sleeping at the Hill of Faith and the Grotto of Repentance."

Having said these words, he withdrew; but they had reached the heart of Fidelity. He arose in haste, like one awakened from sleep by the cry of the enemy, or of fire, and without delaying a moment, he ran to his servants and awakened them, and bade them watch at their post, while he cried aloud for mercy himself, lying prostrate on the earth. The moon was gone, and the rain fell fast. But Fidelity was quite regardless of it. His Friend had drawn near to him again the moment he had awakened his servants, and had raised his voice in prayer; but owing to the darkness of the night he did not see him.

With the first ray of the morning light he caught a glimpse of him, but it was an imperfect one, for he had hid himself in part behind the thick shade of an olive tree, not choosing at present that Fidelity should discover all the tenderness of his countenance. Yet to see but the skirt of his garment was joy unspeakable to Fidelity. From lamentation his voice changed to thanksgiving; he called out, " Thy loving-kindness is better than life; my lips shall praise thee." But soon afterwards he added, " May there yet be hope for a sinner like me ? "

His Friend recalled to his mind, in reply, these sweet words of his Prince: " Come unto me all ye that labor and are heavy laden, and I will give you rest." But my story becomes too long.

The tender and merciful Friend of Fidelity was entreated by him, and he kindly promised to recall his servants. His power opened the prison doors, and set the captives free; and once more they appeared in the garden. Yet they looked dull and unfit for work; and while Fidelity fell at the feet of his Friend, and thanked him for his kindness, a secret feeling of sadness stole over his heart.

His Friend in reply, half hiding his face
with his mantle, said to him, "You will
find very great difficulty in setting your
servants again to work: the fetters with
which they have been confined have so
cramped and injured them, and your own
frame is so enfeebled by that pernicious
food which Profession gave you, that another
wand, as well as that of Diligence, will now
be necessary to enable you to keep your
servants at work." With that he stretched
out to Fidelity a little black wand, by children usually called Correction, but by older
people Affliction.

Fidelity felt his flesh creep, and his servants turned pale at the sight of this rod ;
but he stretched out his trembling hand
and took it, as a token of his Prince's love,
saying, "Both thy rod and thy staff shall
comfort me. But, Lord, how long ? "

When he received the rod, his Friend answered his last question with a smile.

And now Fidelity, with the rod of Affliction, led his servants to the Grotto of Repentance and the Hill of Salvation; and often, as he looked at them working, and remembered his late deliverance, he would, when faint and trembling, kiss his rod, and say, " How far sweeter is this rod to me than the enticing fruit of Sensual Pleasure!"

In a little time the long-suffering Friend of Fidelity took his rod from him; and after his servants had labored well in the Grotto of Repentance, the Mount of Salvation, and the Vineyard of Charity, he took them again to the Arbor of Hope, and played them once again the Melody of Zion.

Thus was Fidelity restored to the ways of peace and obedience. But from time to time his Friend put into his hand the rod of Correction; for he found that it was an extraordinary assistance to him in governing his servants.

After this event, Fidelity felt great uneasiness on account of Profession. He had tenderly loved that boy in former days, and he still earnestly desired his welfare; but he feared to trust himself again in his company. He sometimes sent him messages of love, affectionately exhorting him to prepare for the coming of the Prince. And he was exceedingly urgent with his Friend to rouse and admonish him. But nothing could be obtained from Profession but general expressions of attachment to his Prince, and fair promises that his garden should be in excellent order at his return.

From time to time reports were spread abroad that the King's Son was returning. The reports were sweet to Fidelity, but spread confusion and disorder among the servants of Profession, who, however, soon returned to their former state of self-indulgence and indifference to the Prince's commands.

Some time had now passed away since the Prince had left the island. By means of his kind friend, and the rods of Affliction and Diligence, which he had given him, there was a great peace in the garden of Fidelity. All the servants knew their posts, and in general loved them.

Fidelity, leaning on the arm of his Beloved, and walking from one part of his garden to another, visiting each in his turn, or, as occasion required, exhorting and disciplining his servants, tasted a peace which the world can neither give nor take away; yet he rejoiced with trembling; he remembered his infirmity, and was humble.

Profession, on the other hand, vainly boasted of his love and attachment to his Prince; yet he cared not that any one should see his garden, for it was empty and desolate. His servants were now entirely settled in the Land of Carnal Desire and Natural Pride.

While things were in this state, early one morning after Fidelity had been watching with his servants at the Hill of Faith and the Grotto of Penitence, he passed through the Vineyard of Love, and ascending the hill, accompanied by his Friend, he sat down in the Arbor of Hope. After taking a view of the lovely prospect seen from thence, and delighting himself with the idea that that heavenly country, the skirts of which he saw, might soon, through the love of his Prince, be his, he thought he saw something moving at a great distance upon the sea. It came from the dominions of his Prince. It drew nearer. It soon appeared to be a fleet of ships. It approached the island. It was soon near enough for Fidelity to perceive that it was a large fleet, formed in the shape of a crescent. In a little while there appeared in the middle of this crescent a single ship, helm and prow gilt with gold, sparkling like the sun. On the helm appeared a canopy, studded with precious stones; beneath it, no doubt, sat the Prince himself. Round this boat were numerous others, of different colors, with rowers variously clad. From these smaller boats proceeded sounds of shawms and trumpets, harps and cymbals; so that they seemed to be filled with musicians.

The ships which formed half of the crescent had each large white flags, which played in the wind and shone brightly in the sun. And as they approached nearer, certain words were discerned written upon a white standard in the middle of this right-hand half of the fleet, and these words were PEACE.

The other half of the fleet had black or fiery-colored flags; and on their standards was written JUDGMENT.

When Fidelity clearly saw these things, and understood that his Prince was coming, he felt a secret joy, which he could not express; but in a few moments the remembrance of his ingratitude to his Prince rushed into his mind, and he trembled, and exclaimed, " Woe is me! how shall I stand before my Prince ?"

The friend who was with him bade him call to mind the love he had received from his Prince in former days, and led him with his servants (all now gathering round him, except a few who still remained in the arbor), to the Grotto and the foot of the Mount of Salvation; and here they lay, crying, " Mercy! mercy!"

Meanwhile, Profession, who was aware of his Master's approach, all hurry and confusion, called his servants together; but, alas! though he called loud and long, the greater part heard not; for one named Worldy Prudence, a person of great renown in the Land of Natural Pride, had sent them down to dig ore in a golden mine called Covetousness, where they could not hear his voice. The few he could assemble together he set to prune the trees in the garden, with some sickles he had bought from a person in their own country called Reformation ; and a few picked up some dead leaves in the Vineyard of Charity. But neither he nor his servants bethought themselves of the Grotto of Repentance, or the Mount of Faith, or of the friend whom their Prince had promised should be their guide and assistant. Yet he endeavored to fill himself with hopes that all would still do well ; and looking up and down the garden, he said, "I have seen many gardens more neglected than mine : and, considering how many difficulties I have had to contend with, I think it is in as good order as can be expected."

The fleet was now very near the land, when the Prince gave orders to cast anchor, and sent forward a herald to proclaim that

5

some of the King's friends were coming speedily to take account of his servants, and to convey such as he judged faithful to the King's own fleet, to be comforted and refreshed after their labors, and to bind in chains of darkness the idle and unfaithful servants, and carry them whither they would not.

When Fidelity heard the words of the herald, he remembered again his own sin, and the love of his Prince, and his heart smote him; but he called to his servants to draw still nearer to the cross.

Profession secretly trembled at the words of the herald, yet still flattered himself with deceitful hopes.

The herald was soon followed by the friends of the King. Each of the servants was called to give an account of his stewardship, and their several dooms appointed; it remained only to decide the fate of Profession and Fidelity.

The footsteps of the King's friends were now heard, as they descended from the hall of the palace into the gardens. They approached towards Fidelity as he lay prostrate at the foot of the cross, surrounded by his servants. "We are vile and ungrateful rebels," said Fidelity; "*we are unprofitable servants. We have sinned against Heaven and in thy sight.*"

"Rise up, my son," they answered. "Your Prince has set his love upon you, and he is your beloved. We see by the employment of your servants *who* has been your guide and director, and your familiar friend; and whom *he* takes sweet counsel with is ever the beloved of your Prince. Your Prince has loved you with an everlasting love. He forgives your rebellion, and sends for you to his own presence."

They then raised him up, and led him by the hand to the sea-shore. His Friend also went with him to the brink. A slen-

der boat waited for him, and he was soon
conveyed to the fleet with the white flag.

Multitudes of the King's servants welcomed him on board. Trumpets and
shawms, cymbals and harps, sounded with
joy; bells, also, were faintly heard from
the happy land, the Land of Glory, where
Fidelity was to be taken.

When the friends of the King had brought
Fidelity to the fleet, they returned to the
garden of Profession. He advanced to
meet them, leaning on the arm of one Self-
Righteousness, who had come from the
Land of Natural Pride to assist him, hearing of his perplexity.

"Where are your servants?" said the
friends of the King. "Your garden is des-
olate; the Hill of Faith and the Grotto of
Repentance are forsaken; the Vineyard of
Charity is uncultivated; and the Arbor of
Hope is overgrown with thorns."

"The work was difficult," replied Profession, letting go the arm of Self-Right-eousness.

"But you might have had assistance."

"Allow me a little more time," replied Profession, in a faltering voice.

"The acceptable time is gone; the day of salvation is forever past," replied the friends of the King; and, binding Profession hand and foot, they led him to the sea-shore, where he was placed in a boat similar to that which carried away Fidelity. But this boat conducted him to the left-hand side of the fleet; and that part of the fleet setting sail quickly, bore him away to a land of unutterable darkness, where the pleasant light of the sun never shineth, where despair casteth out hope, and death's everlasting agonies consume the inhabitants.

The fleet with the white flag soon also set sail; but not before Fidelity had been brought into the presence of his Prince, and cast at his feet a garment of immortal amaranth which had been given him. He was clothed with celestial garments, and his countenance glowed with renovated youth and beauty. His Prince received him with tender love, and comforted him with the words of heavenly consolation.

Then the fleet set sail, turning its course to the Land of eternal Love ; and the heavenly symphony of the musicians sounded faintly and more faintly from the departing fleet.

By the command of the Prince, a pillar of white marble was erected in the gardens of Profession and Fidelity, for the benefit of those who might afterwards possess them. On the pillar in the garden of Fidelity was inscribed :

EVERY

THOUGHT MUST BE

BROUGHT INTO CAPTIVITY TO

THE OBEDIENCE OF

CHRIST.

On that in the garden of Profession was inscribed :

EVERY

IMAGINATION OF THE

THOUGHT OF MAN'S HEART IS

ONLY EVIL CONTINU-

ALLY.

O ye young ones, who read the story of Fidelity and Profession, learn hence to restrain your busy, active, wandering thoughts. Teach them to labor at the Grotto of Repentance, the Hill of Faith, the Vineyard of Charity, and the Arbor of Hope. But attempt not the work in your own strength ; you have a Friend who loves you tenderly, who will help you, strengthen you, comfort you, and who has promised never to leave you ; in his strong help go forth, and you will assuredly go forth to success, to victory, and to glory.

ANNE AND FRANK.

ANNE AND FRANK.

CHAPTER I.

"MAMMA," cried Anne, as she came running into the room where her mother was sitting, one beautiful day in September, "only see what Frank and I have found in the woods!" and she held up a basket of fine wild grapes.

"They are really quite a prize, my darling," said Mrs. Morris; "where did you get them?"

"Why, mamma, as we were coming home from school we met Charley Green, and he wanted us to go round with him through the woods—it was not much farther, he said; so I thought you would be willing, for you told us we might be out till dinner-time. Well, just as we got down by that pretty little brook, you know, I happened to look up, and saw such clusters of beautiful purple grapes peeping from among the green leaves right over our heads. So I remembered that I heard you say you wished you could find some to make grape-jelly for poor Susan Ellis, and I thought I would fill my lunch-basket with them, and Frank has got his full too. Now, mamma, when you have made the jelly, may we not carry it to Susan?"

"Yes, my darling, you have certainly earned that pleasure, and I am glad you are so ready to think of the poor and sick. And now, as you have a little time to spare, you may come and read to me from your new book, while Frank is feeding his chickens."

While Anne is reading, we will take the opportunity to give our little readers some account of the children whom we have just

introduced to them. Anne and Frank
Morris had lost their father long before
they could remember, and they now lived
with their mamma in the pleasant country
village of B—. Their house was very prettily situated on a rising ground, and from its
front windows you might see in the distance the beautiful M— river. It was very
pleasant now and then to catch a glimpse
of a white sail on its blue waters. Not far
off, the pleasant country church stood on a
green, quite by itself, with a pretty chapel
at its side, and a little gem of a parsonage
opposite.

Anne was a dark-eyed, quiet little girl,
about eight years old, very fond of reading,
but a great lover of play too, especially
when she and Frank were together; for
Frank, I am sorry to say, seldom took up
a book out of school-hours, except when his
mamma would allow him to read a few
pages aloud to her. Even then, if he heard

Dash bark, or saw a boy flying a kite in the street, down would go the book, and he would be off before you knew it; for Frank was a firm believer in the old saying, " All work and no play makes Jack a dull boy; " and his books would have been much oftener found, when he wanted them, on the stairs or on the hall-floor, than on the shelf where they belonged, if his mamma had not watched him very closely.

These children went to school, but in summer they had a very long vacation — so long that they did not know what to do with themselves, and were very glad when their mamma proposed to teach them for an hour or two every morning. So, after breakfast was over, and they had taken a nice walk with mamma and Dash, they would take their books and work, if the weather was fine, under one of the trees in the orchard, or if not, into their pleasant play-room, and so spend the morning very

happily; while Dash lay at their feet brush-
ing off the flies with his tail, and looking as
if he wondered why he could not have
some lessons too. Occasionally Master
Frank would be detected in gathering a
flower, or tying a piece of grass round
Dash's tail, when he should have been
studying his spelling-lessons, and on the
whole the studies did not progress quite so
well in the garden as they did in the house.
The children were very much pleased, when
they had studied their lessons well, to be
permitted as a reward to go and visit their
grandmother, who lived in the same village.
Grandma had been ill for several years,
and scarcely ever left the house; but she
loved her little grandchildren dearly, and
always had a kind word and a pleasant
smile for them. Many were the happy
hours which Anne and Frank spent with
this dear friend, listening to the delightful
stories with which she would entertain and

instruct them, inventing tale after tale with
a talent peculiarly her own, and drawing
from each some beautiful lesson which they
could easily understand and practise. And
when they could no longer listen to the
words of instruction from those lips, and
when the eyes which had so often beamed
upon them in love were closed in the sleep
of death, those stories and the beautiful
lessons which they conveyed were still remembered.

" Mamma," said Anne, after she had
done reading, and had sat for some time
quite thoughtful, with her book in her
hand, " isn't to-morrow communion Sunday ? "

" Yes, dear, it is.   But why do you ask
the question ? "

" Why, mamma, I was thinking what
communion Sunday could mean.   Frank
and I have often talked about it, and we
can't understand it at all.   You know you

Home.

Charley, p. 81.

always want us to ask you about anything that we cannot understand."

"I am very glad, my darling," said Mrs. Morris, "that you have asked this question, because it shows you have thought about it; and I think you are now old enough to understand something of this subject. To-morrow evening we will spend the hour after tea, which, you know, is always yours, in talking about it. In the meantime, I wish you to remember what a sacred and solemn service it is, and to behave with propriety all the time, not laughing or trifling, but giving your whole attention to it."

6

CHAPTER II.

ANNE and Frank were up bright and early the next morning, for it was a rule in the family of Mrs. Morris that the breakfast-hour should be no later on Sunday mornings than on week days. She could see no reason why we do not need as long a day to serve God as to attend to our worldly business; and besides, as the day is observed in memory of our Saviour's resurrection, the early morning hour, when he burst the bonds of death, is the one best calculated to remind us of him.

The children loved to rise early on this blessed day, and when Anne was a very little girl, her mamma would sometimes be awakened on Sabbath morning by her pleasant little voice singing —

"This is the day when Christ arose
So early from the dead!
Why should we keep our eyelids closed,
And waste our hours in bed?"

When they had eaten their breakfast, and
were all ready for Sunday-school, they sat
down to look over their lessons which had
been learned the evening before till it was
time for the bell to ring. They were very
careful not to be late, for they knew what
a disturbance it makes when children are
late at Sunday-school ; and it is always best
to be there as soon as the services com-
mence. Their mamma gave them a great
many lessons about behaving well during
the services in church, but I am sorry to
say they did not always remember them.
During the sermon there was many a stolen
peep at the *Well-spring* or library-book,
and a restlessness and inattention far from
proper. Children, as well as grown persons, ought to realize far more than they

do the sacredness of the house of God. It would be well if they were taught by the example of those who are older to enter the sanctuary in a quiet, solemn manner, to engage reverently in the services, and not to leave it with indecent haste. It is painful to see, as we often do, the whole congregation remain seated, without even the appearance of reverence, while their pastor is addressing the throne of grace. Surely the outward signs of respect which would be observed in the presence of an earthly monarch ought to be remembered in the presence of the King of kings.

I am happy to say that Anne remembered what her mamma had told her about trifling during the communion-service, and that she had talked to Frank about it. They both behaved with great propriety that day, and their mamma was very much gratified to see it. That Sabbath was a very pleasant one to them, because they had tried to spend it as they ought. After tea, when they had, as usual, said their catechism and hymns, Anne reminded her mamma of her promise.

"I have not forgotten it, my darling," replied Mrs. Morris, "and I am always happy to gratify you, specially when I see you trying to do right, as you have been to-day." So they drew their chairs near the open door leading into the garden, and their mamma thus began:

"Many years ago there lived in a remote part of this state a gentleman whom I shall call Mr. Murray. His house stood on the declivity of a hill, commanding a fine view of a pretty village below, with the distant blue mountains beyond, while on the other side you might see the glittering towers and spires of the neighboring city, with its noble harbor, and the wide ocean stretching as far as the eye could reach. There was a farm of many acres connected with the home stead, and at the foot of the hill, under a magnificent elm tree, stood the quiet farmhouse, not the least attractive object in the landscape. A beautiful lawn sloped down from the house to the graceful avenue which led to its entrance from the street, and behind, rising towards the summit of the hill, were the garden and orchard, the latter communicating with the house by a glass door opening into the library. Mr. Murray had a family of five or six children, boys and girls, and very happy they were in their beautiful home. Every season of the year brought its own pleasures. In summer, they loved to play in the beautiful woods and groves which surrounded their home ; to tumble about in the new-mown hay, run races in the garden, or climb the trees in the orchard. Occasionally they would be allowed to drive in their little pony-carriage to the neighboring village, to carry some nice little thing for their mamma to a sick person, and it made them very happy to feel that they could be useful in this way.

"Winter, too, brought its own enjoyments,—coasting, sliding, and snow-balling, —and the first snow storm was always welcomed with a shout of delight. Then the merry sleighrides to and from school, with an occasional upset in a snow bank, by way of adventure ; and the long, cheerful evenings, when they would gather round the warm fire and blazing lamp, while their mamma would assist them in studying their lessons for the next day, and encourage them by the promise of reading to them from some favorite book as soon as they were finished. These were pleasant hours, and long to be remembered.

"But a change came over the prospects of this happy family. Mr. Murray had for some time been unsuccessful in business, and had of late been induced by the imprudent advice of friends to engage in some rash speculations which proved unfortunate, and which occasioned the loss of nearly all his property. It was with a sad heart that he announced to his family the melancholy intelligence that they must leave the beautiful home so dear to them all, for he could no longer in justice retain it.

"Those only who have been called to leave a happy home can imagine the feelings of these children as they wandered over every spot endeared to them by pleasant memories, — how they lingered in the garden, the orchard, the grove, — and as they gazed on the blossoming trees which filled the air with fragrance, wondered who would gather their delicious fruit. Nor did Mr. and Mrs. Murray part with less regret from the birthplace of their children, — a spot where they had spent so many happy hours.

"On the final settlement of Mr. Murray's affairs, it was found that after his debts were paid scarcely enough would remain to support his family, with the strictest economy. They removed immediately to a small house in the neighboring city, where Mr. Murray struggled hard to reëstablish himself in business, and his wife and children strove by every means in their power to soothe and encourage him. But they sorely missed their happy home, and all the country pleasures to which they had so long been accustomed. Mr. and Mrs. Murray could bear the loss of their own comforts with comparative cheerfulness, but the tears often filled their eyes as they watched the rosy cheeks of their children becoming paler, and their steps less elastic, from day to day."

Here Mrs. Morris paused, and Frank, looking up, with a tear in his bright eye, exclaimed, "O mamma, is that all, and did they never get back to their beautiful home ? "

" That I cannot tell you, my dear," said Mrs. Morris ; " for this is the end of my story. But now I want you to give me your attention, while I try to explain the reason why I have told it to you."

The children drew closer to their mother, and looked up earnestly in her face.

" Suppose, my darlings," she said, " that some kind friend of Mr. Murray, who was very wealthy, hearing of his troubles, had generously come forward and offered to pay his debts, so that he and his family could return to their happy home. Now, place yourselves in the situation of that family, and tell me how you should think they would feel towards that kind friend."

" Oh ! " cried both children at once, " they would feel as if they could never love him enough, or do half enough for him."

" And suppose that, in order to do all this, this kind friend had been obliged to leave his own pleasant home, to become very poor — to suffer a great deal, and at last to lose his life. Suppose that just before his death he had asked the friends for whom he had done so much to remember and think of him at some particular time, would they not gladly comply with his last request ? "

Frank looked very thoughtful, and Anne, raising her eyes, filled with tears, to her mother's face, said : " Mamma, I begin now to see why you have told us this story."

" I am very glad you do, my dear little girl," said Mrs. Morris, as she stooped and kissed her cheek ; " but what I have told you can give you but a very, very faint idea of what the Lord Jesus Christ has done for us. What is the loss of an earthly home, however beautiful, compared with that of a

heavenly home? What is all the kindness
of an earthly friend compared with the con-
descension of the Son of God himself, who
left the glories of heaven, and became an
infant, born in a manger, having no place
to lay his head, and after a life of suffering
died a painful death, and endured, instead
of us, the punishment which we had de-
served? And if we knew what were the
last wishes of such a friend, should we not
wish to remember them? Take your little
Bible, Frank, and read to us from the
twenty-third to the twenty-sixth verses of
the eleventh chapter of the first epistle to
the Corinthians."

Frank read, slowly and distinctly, the
following verses:

"The Lord Jesus, the same night in
which he was betrayed, took bread, and
when he had given thanks, he brake it, and
said, Take, eat; this is my body which is
broken for you: this do in remembrance of

me. After the same manner, also, he took
the cup, when he had supped, saying, This
cup is the New Testament in my blood;
this do ye, as oft as ye drink it, in remembrance of me. For as often as ye eat this
bread, and drink this cup, ye do show the
Lord's death till he come."

"Now do you not see," continued Mrs.
Morris, "that when Christians meet together to eat this bread and to drink this
wine, they do it in remembrance of Him
who loved them so much? The bread re-
minds them of his body, and the wine of
his blood. You know, as I have often told
you, that we have very wicked hearts, and
should not love our Saviour at all if these
hearts were not changed. And even after
we have begun to love him, we are still so
wicked that we should often forget how
much he has done for us if we did not have
something to remind us of it. And when
we keep the communion, or the Lord's

Supper, Jesus Christ himself is there with us just as much as if we could see him, helping us to remember his love to us, and to learn to be like him, — teaching us to hate the sin which caused him to suffer so much, and resolve that, with the help of his Holy Spirit, we will try to follow his example, and become every day more and more like Jesus. May you, my dear children, be washed from your sins in his precious blood, that you may feel how much you owe to him, and love to join with others in keeping his last commandment."

CHAPTER III.

ANNE and Frank had not forgotten the promised visit to Susan Ellis, and the first half-holiday was fixed upon for it. Susan lived several miles from the village, and the children always looked forward with delight to the pleasant drive through the woods to her house. But on this day the quick eye of the mother noticed that Frank seemed less interested about it than Anne, and that he looked rather thoughtful. She inquired the reason.

"Why, mamma," he said, "you know we were to have our cricket-match this afternoon that we have been so long getting up, and our uniforms are just done, and it is such a beautiful day."

"Well, my boy, what then? I am sure

we do not wish you to go with us unless
you like; and if you had rather join the
cricket-match, Anne and I will visit Susan
alone."

Frank hesitated. "I am not quite sure,
mamma, what I ought to do about it. It is
a long time since we have seen Susan, and
she thinks so much of our coming; and —
and — I am afraid it would be selfish to
prefer my own pleasure to hers."

Mrs. Morris did not immediately reply.
She knew her boy was thinking of the verse
he had repeated that morning,—"Look not
every man on his own things, but every man
also on the things of others," — and she
could not but offer a silent thanksgiving to
Him who had thus led him to make His
Word "the man of his counsel." "I wish
you to decide this question for yourself,
Frank," she said, at last. "We shall not
go till three o'clock, and that will give you
plenty of time."

The carriage was at the door just as the clock struck three. Anne and her mother were all ready to start, but Frank was nowhere to be found. Mrs. Morris looked disappointed, though she said nothing; but just as they were stepping into the carriage, they saw him running towards them very fast, from one of the neighboring houses.

"I have just been to tell Andrew Murray I could not go to the cricket-match," he said, almost out of breath. "I am so glad I am not too late."

What a pleasant drive that was! It was a most lovely afternoon. There was not a cloud in the sky, and the air had all that delicious softness peculiar to early autumn. When they had left the village, Frank begged to be allowed to drive, to which John, who was very good-natured, consented. Katy seemed to know her little master's hand; for she pricked up her ears, tossed

7

her head proudly, and trotted off in fine
style, as if to do credit to his driving,
while Dash raced along in his own inde-
pendent manner, now darting across the
fields in chase of a squirrel, and then running back to see how his friend Katy was
getting along. The woods were fragrant
with the smell of the pine: the blue gen-
tian and wild aster grew in abundance by
the wayside, frequently tempting the children to stop and gather a bouquet for their
mother, and at the same time bring to the
carriage a handful of fine blackberries.

The cottage of Susan Ellis stood just at
the end of these woods. It was small and
unpainted, but everything about it showed
marks of neatness and order. As they drove
up to the door, it was opened by a mid-
dle-aged woman, neatly dressed, and with
a very pleasant face, who gave them a cordial welcome. To the inquiry of Mrs.
Morris, " How is your sister to-day, Mrs.

Hammond ? " she replied, " Ah, ma'am, poor Susan has had another of her ill turns, and has not been able to speak for several days. But she will be very glad to see you. Will you walk up ? "

While John was taking from the carriage various supplies of tea, sugar, etc., which Mrs. Morris had thought might be needed in the family, the party followed Mrs. Hammond up the narrow staircase into the room above. Poor Susan lay on her bed, partly supported by pillows, her face almost as white as their snowy covering. She met them with a pleasant smile, though unable to speak. She had been for fifteen years confined to that bed, suffering frequently from terrible spasms, which often left her speechless for weeks together. Yet she was cheerful and happy, and loved to surround herself with pleasant things. Her windows were full of beautiful plants — bright geraniums and fragrant heliotropes — and among them hung cages filled with beautiful canary birds, most of which she had raised herself, and which, with their sweet songs, cheered many of her weary hours. Susan enjoyed very much the visits of children, and loved to hear their merry voices in her pleasant room. She was very glad to see Anne and Frank, and was much gratified with their little present. It was indeed most acceptable, for fruit and jellies were almost the only things she was able to eat. Taking down a slate and pencil which hung by her bedside, she began to converse with the children, asking them questions about their school, their plays, etc., and telling them little things which she thought might interest them. Then bidding them go and look at her birds and flowers, she directed her conversation to Mrs. Morris, answering cheerfully her kind inquiries after her health, and alluding with gratitude to the mercies which she enjoyed.

"I lie here," she wrote, "hour after hour, enjoying the sweet air which comes in at the open window, listening to the merry voices of my sister's children as they gather the apples in the orchard, and think of the goodness of Him who has thus surrounded us with beauty and plenty. It has pleased him to call me to suffer, but I know he has a wise and merciful design in it, and I think I can say from my heart, ' Blessed is that sorrow, however severe, which leads me one step nearer to my Father's throne.' "

As they rose to take leave, she beckoned the children nearer to her side, and laid her hand solemnly on their heads. Then taking her pencil, she wrote, "May the God of your parents be your God, my dear children. May He to whom you were consecrated in baptism own the seal of his covenant, and call you early into his fold."

The children were quite silent and

thoughtful on their way home. At last Anne said: "Mamma, what did Susan mean by calling our baptism the seal of God's covenant? I know we were baptized when we were babies, but I never thought much about what it meant."

"That will be an interesting subject for our next Sunday evening's talk, Anne," replied her mother. "In the meantime, I wish you would be thinking about it as much as you can, for it is a subject I want you to understand."

"Mamma," said Frank, after a short pause, "did you not say that Susan had been as ill as she is now ever since I was born?"

"Yes, my boy, and for many years before that. When I first knew her she was a blooming, healthy girl of nineteen, and was living in the family of a friend of mine in the neighborhood of Boston. One very hot day in summer, having worked hard,

and being much heated, she very impru-
dently went down cellar, and drank freely
of iced milk. The sudden check of per-
spiration threw her into violent distress, and
from the effects of that illness she never
entirely recovered. The excellent lady
with whom she had lived always treated
her with the utmost kindness, and had
taken great pains to give her religious instruction, frequently reading to her, as she
sat at work, from the Bible and other good
books, and explaining them to her. Susan
never forgot what she learned there, and it
has been a great comfort to her through
her illness. Mrs. Manners did everything
she could for her, and procured her the
best medical advice; but it was all of no
use. She has provided her with every comfort, and scarcely a week passes that she or
her children do not visit her."

As they drew nearer to the village,
merry shouts reminded the party that they

were approaching the cricket-ground. The game was over, and the boys were scattered in groups among the trees, their red and white uniforms contrasting very prettily with the slightly changing foliage. Some of them caught sight of Frank, and greeted him with three loud cheers, which he heartily returned, and as he turned to his mother, the bright smile on his face assured her that he did not regret the manner in which he had spent the afternoon.

CHAPTER IV.

It so happened that on the next Sabbath several parents presented their children for baptism, and among others was a sister of Mrs. Morris. The children were delighted with the prospect of witnessing the interesting ceremony, and it was difficult to keep their attention from wandering to their sweet little baby cousin, as she slept in her nurse's arms by their side. But they had heard much about baptism, and wondered what it meant, and they looked on with great interest, while Mr. Howard sprinkled water on the foreheads of the little children, and, calling them by name, solemnly pronounced the words, " I baptize thee into the name of the Father, and of the Son, and of the Holy Ghost."

They listened, and tried to understand, while he earnestly prayed that the little ones thus publicly given to the Saviour might be his indeed; that their parents might remember that they were a charge intrusted to them by their heavenly Father, to be trained up for him; that if their lives were spared they might give their hearts to that Saviour to whom they had thus been consecrated.

The service was over, and the children walked home thoughtfully by their mother's side. At the usual hour for evening conversation, they gladly seated themselves at the little door leading into the garden, and Anne began by asking —

"Mamma, why did Mr. and Mrs. Jefferson wait so long before they had their children baptized? Helen is five years old, and Freddy nearly three. I thought all children were baptized when they were babies?"

'Do you not remember, my dear, that last Sabbath Mr. and Mrs. Jefferson were admitted to the communion of the church?"

"Yes, mamma."

"Did you know what they meant when they stood at the altar and acknowledged the covenant which Mr. Howard read?"

"Not exactly."

"They have lately been brought by the Spirit of God to see their need of a Saviour, and since they began to realize how much they owe to him, they have felt that they could never do enough to show their gratitude. They never thought much about this before, but now it is their wish to give up themselves and everything they have to the service of their Redeemer, and they have made a solemn public promise to do so. And now they are anxious to give up their children also to God; and as they find in their Bible that precious promise, 'I will be a God to thee, and to thy seed after thee,' they have, in this public manner, acknowledged that they believe that promise, and desire that God should take their children to be his, and be their God. They promise to bring them up for him, and God promises to bless them if they do so; and this is what we call the baptismal covenant."

"But does not God bless any children except those who are baptized?" asked Frank.

"Yes, my dear; you know he says, 'Suffer little children to come unto me, and forbid them not, for of such is the kingdom of heaven.' I wish you would listen to me, and try to understand this. You remember that God told Adam that if he disobeyed him he would bring misery on all his children. Adam did disobey; and as we are all sinners, there would be no hope for any of us if Jesus Christ had not borne the punishment of our sins, and died that we might be saved. Now if a little child dies before it is old enough to learn of a Saviour, whether it has been baptized or not, Christ will wash it in his own blood, and take it to himself in heaven. But it is the duty of every Christian parent to have his children baptized, because baptism is a sign that the child must be washed from sin, and that God takes it as his own by covenant. A child that has been baptized belongs particularly to Christ and to his church, in a way which other children do not; and all Christians feel, or ought to feel, a particular interest in those children who belong to them by baptism. Now, if such a child given to God, and faithfully instructed by its parents, forsakes that Saviour to whom it has been consecrated, and wanders into sinful ways, is it not more to blame than children who have not been baptized?"

"Yes, mamma," answered both children, seriously.

"Then, my darlings," said Mrs. Morris, laying a hand on the head of each, as they sat by her side, " never forget the solemn promise made for you at your baptism, and which, now that you are old enough, it is your duty to make for yourselves. Give your hearts now to that Saviour to whom your parents then consecrated you, that so the prayers offered for you by your beloved father when he sprinkled upon you the water of baptism may be heard, now that he is gone to dwell with his Saviour forever. Remember that, in the words of that beautiful hymn which you joined in singing this morning —

'The seal of love divine,
The sign of covenant grace you wear.'

And now, Anne, you may call John and Sarah, for it is time for evening prayer."

The little family joined as usual in reading each a few verses from the Holy Word, and then when each had given, according to his ability, an account of the sermons which they had heard that day, a fervent supplication went up from their united hearts to the God of the Sabbath, and their voices joined in the beautiful hymn—

> " My God, how endless is thy love!
>   Thy gifts are every evening new,
>   And morning mercies from above
>   Gently distil like early dew.
>
> " Thou spread'st the curtain of the night,
>   Great Guardian of my sleeping hours;
>   Thy sovereign word restores the light,
>   And quickens all my drowsy powers.
>
> " I yield my powers to thy command,
>   To thee I consecrate my days;
>   Perpetual blessings from thy hand,
>   Demand perpetual songs of praise."

CHAPTER V.

October, with its bright, clear days, its ripening harvests and brilliant foliage, was rapidly passing away. The delicate annuals in the children's little gardens had yielded to the frost, and breathed out their short lives of beauty and fragrance, to bloom again with the return of spring. The roses, geraniums, and heliotropes had been transplanted into pots, and removed to the house, to cheer by their presence the dark days and long evenings of winter. Yet autumn brought its own pleasures,— the long ride to the orchard in the empty apple-cart, and the merry shouts that hailed its return after a busy afternoon, loaded with the red and yellow fruit ; the search among the dry leaves for nuts, when a high wind had saved Frank the trouble of climbing into the tree to shake them off; and the pleasant walks which their mamma loved to take with them in this clear, bracing weather.

It was fine weather for studying, too, and Anne and Frank were very busy preparing for the examination. There were no prizes to be distributed among those who had been most successful; but when the day arrived, and the children proved by the promptness and intelligence of their answers that they had really understood the lessons which they had learned, the approving smile of their teacher, and the affectionate kiss and words of encouragement which awaited them at home, were a sufficient reward for all their efforts.

Thanksgiving was now very near, and how delightful it was to look forward to the two weeks' vacation, which they were to pass at the house of their kind uncle — the home

of their own mother's childhood! How
they loved to hear from her lips pleasant
stories about every spot in and around that
dear old house! In summer they loved to
walk with her up the green lane which led
to the pretty cottage where she used to go
to school when a very little child, and she
would tell them of the prim schoolmistress
who always sat in the corner, with her
work-basket at her side, and beside it the
dreaded fool's cap, which generally found
its way to the head of some naughty little
boy or girl before school was done; of the
pleasant play-ground, near which stood an
old, old house, and at its window there sat
a dear old lady in a mob-cap and neat white
apron, who loved to hear the merry voices
of the children, often calling them to her
and giving them some nice fruit, and sometimes inviting them into the house and
showing them the wonderful curiosities in
the old-fashioned parlor. Then there was

the beautiful grove behind the house, with
the pretty pond where they loved to sail
their boats; the hill, which seemed made on
purpose for them to run down its green
slope; and the rocks which they used to
call their grotto. How many pleasant
things their mamma could remember about
this grove! — the lovely Sabbath evenings,
when she and her brothers and sisters would
come there with their parents, and, seated
on those rocks, repeat the good old Assem-
bly's Catechism, which was the fashion in
those days; and which was not taught them,
as was the case in too many families, merely
to be repeated like a parrot, but explained
to them as far as they could understand it,
and often illustrated by some interesting
story, which they always afterwards associated with it.

The little party of cousins, assembled to
pass the vacation together, found much to
enjoy though the warm summer days were

past, the garden had begun to look desolate,
and the trees were stripped of their foliage.
There were plenty of nuts to be gathered,
and shelled in the evening by the blazing
wood fire.   There was the corn, too, to be
husked; and though the busy little fingers
could not help much, the bright, merry
faces were always welcome in the barn.
Then there were the colt, the calf, and
especially the donkey, which last little animal was a never-ending source of amuse-
ment.   Scarcely a day passed that did not
see him harnessed to his little green cart,
and trudging to the village post-office, at a
pace which not all the shouts and efforts of
his little drivers could urge beyond a sober
jog-trot.   Yet Jack was a very useful little
animal, and was the means of accomplishing
a great deal of good, though he did not know
much about it himself.   The little green
cart might often be seen at the doors of the
neighboring cottages, laden with supplies

for Thanksgiving ; for the children had been taught that the best way to show our gratitude for our own blessings is to do all we can to relieve the wants of others, and the hearts of many a poor family were cheered by the smiles and kind words of their little visitors, as well as by the substantial gifts which they brought from their parents.

Thanksgiving Day ! How many pleasant recollections are associated with that name — a name as dear to us as Christmas to old England. Thanksgiving and Christmas ! Let us never cease to remember those days — the one set apart by our pious fathers for a thankful acknowledgment of all our mercies, and especially of that richest gift of Heaven, a Divine Redeemer ; the other, consecrated to the remembrance of that Redeemer's birth.

With grateful hearts, the happy family-circle welcomed the return of this joyous day. There were vacant seats at the fire-

side, and they could not but sigh as they
thought of the loved ones whom they should
meet no more on earth ; but why should
they mourn for those who had only gone
before them to their Father's house in
heaven? There was much—oh, how much!
—cause for gratitude as they thought of the
many blessings which had followed them
since last they met around that fireside, and
they gladly obeyed the summons which
called them to offer the sacrifice of thanksgiving, and to pay their vows to the Lord
in the presence of all his people. Once
more, as in the days of childhood, they
assembled in the church where their parents had worshipped, joined in the public
thanksgiving, and listened to the words of
instruction from the pulpit in which a beloved father had once ministered. And
was there no cause for gratitude that the
hand of modern improvement had as yet
spared that venerable sanctuary, hallowed

by so many memories of the past; that the noble pulpit still stood in its dignified simplicity; that the spacious and comfortable pews had not been exchanged for fashionable slips, and the holy and beautiful house where their fathers had worshipped was still an object with which they could associate all the sweet recollections of childhood? Let those who love the past be forgiven, if they find cause for gratitude in what may appear to some mere sentimentalism.

There was one spot yet to be visited; and the day before their return home, Mrs. Morris led her children to the quiet graveyard where rested all that was mortal of one beloved parent. There, within sight of the home of her infancy, a spot to which she hoped one day to return, she trusted that she and her children should be laid by his side, to await together a glorious resurrection. It was a lovely, retired spot, and close beside its entrance rose a simple monument of gray stone, bearing on one side the name and age of the departed, and on the other the words expressive of the faith of every Christian heart,—" I believe in the communion of saints."

The children stood for some time in silence by their mother's side, till Anne, pointing to the inscription, said, "Are those words in the Bible, mamma? I am sure I have seen them before."

"No, my darling; it is in the prayer-book that you have seen them. They are a part of the 'Apostles' Creed,' which is repeated every Sabbath in the Episcopal church. They are very beautiful words," she added, as they seated themselves on a rustic bench within the enclosure, " and I should like you to understand their meaning. Frank, you know, is soon to leave us, to spend the winter at Mr. Nelson's school. He will have a great deal to enjoy, and a great many things to take up his time; but will he not, when far away among strangers, love to think of his mother and sister? Though he cannot be near me, to show his love, he will try to do so by doing what he thinks will please me, and will look forward with delight to his return home, when he can be with me as you are, and you can together show your love to me. Now we have a great deal to enjoy, and a great many things to think of in this world; but if we love our Saviour as we ought, shall we not love to think of him more than anything else, try to please him, and long for the time to come when we shall be near him? And shall we not think a great deal about our dear friends who loved him on earth, and are now gone to be with him forever? And may we not suppose that they are thinking of us, and longing for the time to come when we shall be near him, as they are, and never be separated any more?

But if we really hope to meet them there, we must love our Saviour as they do, and show that we do so by keeping his commandments. Let us remember, my dear children, as we visit this grave, that if we wish to meet your dear father in the presence of our Saviour, we must become followers of him, as he followed Christ."